May 2023

To Kelly and your little one —

I hope you enjoy my book, and know that myself and many others have flourished under the teachings and inspiration of your grandmother, Grace Koopmans.

One stance she believed in was that animals should and speak in books. I have followed her thinking in my story yet downplayed the Wolfhound's kindness, thoughtfulness and bravery.

Joann Lahm Jackson

P.S. Jim Bgrrow — I knew her 60 years ago.

Adventures of a Wolfhound and the Leprechauns

WRITTEN BY
JoAnn Lakin Jackson
ILLUSTRATED BY
Katherine J. Moloney

©2022 by JoAnn Lakin Jackson

All rights reserved. No part of this publication may be reproduced or transmitted in any form or by any means, electronic or mechanical, including photocopying, recording, or any other information storage and retrieval system, without the written permission of the author or publisher.

This book is a work of fiction. All of the names, characters, events, and incidents in this book are a product of the author's imagination. Any resemblance to actual persons or events is purely coincidental and not intentional.

Printed in the United States of America

Published in Hellertown, PA

Adventures of a Wolfhound and Leprechauns
by JoAnn Lakin Jackson

Illustrated by Katherine J. Moloney
Photo on page 33 by Kathy Crow
Cover by Christina Gaugler

34 p. , ill., 21.5mm x 28mm

ISBN: 978-0-916262-20-4

PZ7.K8174 BL

SUBJECTS: Ireland—Folklore—Fiction, Irish Wolfhounds Ireland—Folklore—Fiction, Leprechauns

Dewey class no. 823.912

2 4 6 8 10 9 7 5 3 1

For more information or to place bulk orders, contact the publisher at Jennifer@BrightCommunications.net.

BrightCommunications.net

To some of the most special creatures to ever walk the Earth, who showed me so many things:

Moira—how calm and loving the wolfhound is

Brynna—the spirit of the hunter in the wolfhound and the independence within

MacLir—that kindness and gentleness are paramount in the wolfhound heart

Gracie—that loving everyone, especially children, is a wonderful adventure

Dori—that loyalty and love are first

Eala—that caring for the young, both human and canine, is first

Michael—that the essence of romance and guardianship as a knight of old lives within the heart of a wolfhound

Connery—that loyalty, humor, and tolerance abide in the spirit

PREFACE

In a time before there were any countries, towns, or cities, people wandered from place to place as do the deer. There were no freeways, roads, or trails. There were no signs to tell them where they were going, only familiar landmarks to tell where they were.

Many things you and I take for granted had not yet been invented—not even the wheel. After a great while, people started to live together in small groups for protection from wild animals. There were wolves, bears, boar, and many kinds of large, wild cats. There were many animals that man feared but found ways to hunt. They would hunt many of them for their fur, which would keep them warm in winter, or to eat them.

It came to be that some wolflike animals became companions to man. One animal that began to be a friend to man was called a wolfdog. He was great protection from many of the animals man feared, as well as a companion in hunting when the people needed food or clothing. These wolfdogs were great in size. They ranged from 30 to 36 inches at the shoulder, and when they stood on their hind feet, they were taller than a man.

A group of people I want to tell you about began to live in the same general area as each other. This group of people was known as Celts. We call them the Celtic people. They did not stay in one place. They slowly moved around, seeking food, and making temporary shelters from whatever they found in each area. They wandered around what is now known as Russia, the Baltic area, Germany, and into what we now know as France. Remember, these people did not have houses yet, and their dogs shared whatever shelter they found or made.

The Celtic people migrated slowly to western France. There they heard of wonderful green lands from the very adventurous men called Vikings. After a while, many of these Celtic people made boats to travel to the west.

These brave Celtic people crossed the sea to what we now call England. Before long, some of the people went north to what we today call Scotland. Others travelled south to where they named Wales, and still others travelled across the sea once more to a land that became known as Ireland.

The time came when people stopped wandering and built homes. The Celts learned that they could grow some of their own food and that cattle were willing to be taken care of. Now the people had milk, food, and clothing. Many inventions were discovered, and life was changing quickly. People had learned to make wheels and carts. They began trading goods and services with each other.

These Celtic people started having rules, forming clans, and choosing leaders who became what we know as royalty. Towns sprang up. There were often arguments over who was in charge. Sometimes they had small wars to decide who would be their leader. Many of the royalty began to build big stone houses we now call castles. Their followers built shelters or homes just outside the castle. The wolfdog lived with these people and still helped with hunting for food and protecting the Celts from wild animals.

The story I am going to tell you is about a wolfdog at this time in history. *Is it true or imaginary?*

One misty, rainy afternoon, a wolfdog was trailing a wild boar. He stopped to smell the air to tell which way the boar had gone.

The wolfdog heard a screeching wee voice yelling, "Get off my foot! Get off my foot!"

The wolfdog looked down, and there was a small, wee man, and—sure enough—the man's foot was caught beneath one of the wolfdog's strong, hairy toes. The great dog carefully lifted his paw, stepped aside, and picked the man up by his shirt with his big, strong teeth and stood the wee man up.

"Tis sure I would turn you into a toad for almost stepping on me, but truth be known, you saved me from the boar. That animal ran off when he saw you were starting to follow him."

The wolfdog sat down with his great paws on either side of the little man. The man's voice was no longer angry.

The dog licked the little fellow, who was no bigger than a wee baby. The sloppy kiss went from tip of his toe to the top of his head.

"You be stopping that now. You'll be drowning me with slobber," said the man, who it turned out was a leprechaun.

The dog looked at the tiny man with curiosity because he knew that leprechauns were known in Ireland to be wee persons full of trickery and magic and to have great wealth.

After the leprechaun stood up and shook himself off, he checked to see if he was all right. He looked up at the great dog and smiled.

"To show you my gratitude for saving my life, I am going to do something for you. I will mark you in a special way so that all who see you will know you are the great hunter that saved me."

The leprechaun went around to each of the wolfdog's hairy paws and touched each one with both hands three times. Before you could blink, the tip of each paw was white.

"From this day on, you and all your progeny will have white toes. If other leprechauns see you, they will know you, your children, and your grandchildren are special ones. All will know of your kindness to me. Remember: If you see a rainbow, surely a leprechaun will be nearby. They would want to use their powers to help you if necessary. All you need to do is ask."

The wolfdog tried to give another kiss, but the leprechaun vanished before he could. Because the boar had run off, the wolfdog returned to the people he lived with.

One day, the wolfdog was out enjoying the spring weather. There had been many rainstorms, so all people and animals had stayed out of the weather.

But now the sun was shining, and it was a great time to just go for a good run.

The dog came upon a small stream he had jumped through many times before. But this time, it was a bigger stream because of all the rain. He wanted to cross, so he was going to have to swim.

Wolfdogs don't find swimming a lot of fun, but they will do so if need be. The wolfdog plunged into the water and began to use his strong, powerful legs. His great head was above the water as was his long tail, which was streaming out behind him. The dog used his tail as a rudder to guide him through the fast-moving water.

As the wolfdog was passing under a fallen tree, he heard a shrill screech. The wolfdog saw a little man—just like the one he had seen before. This wee man had fallen off the log as he was trying to cross the stream.

The dog swam with strong, forceful strokes over to the little man.

"Hold on to my tail," said the wolfdog as he let the leprechaun hold onto his tail. Then the wolfdog towed the little man out of the water to the grassy bank.

The leprechaun was cold and wet, but he was safe.

He saw the white toes on the wolfdog and said, "I have heard of you and your kindness to one of my cousins. You have surely saved me from drowning today. All will know of it because I will mark you in a special way."

With this, the leprechaun touched the dog's tail—but only the very tip of the tail.

"From now on, all will know the wolfdog with the white toes is the brave creature that saved one of our people from the wild boar and now has saved me from the roiling waters. I will mark the very tip of your tail and so you will always show the sign of having been our hero. Your children and grandchildren will also show this mark, which will set them aside as special friends to us," the leprechaun said.

The wolfdog gave the leprechaun a big kiss.

"And always remember, if you see a rainbow, you know a leprechaun is never far away," said the leprechaun.

The leprechaun touched the tip of the wolfdog's tail three times, and then he vanished.

Time passed, and one day the wolfdog went hunting with the people with whom he lived. They took trips to the sea where the wolfdog loved running on the beach with the wind in his face. The wolfdog took great pleasure in running with other wolfdogs on great green grassy rolling hills called the moors.

His was a good life, and he was kind to all he met—except for wolves.

One day as the sun came up, the wolfdog could see this was going to be an especially fine day.

He stretched. His giant paws came forward, and then he wiggled his great, white toes. He arched his back and extended his

great length with his tail straight out behind him—right to the end of his great tail with the white markings on the tip.

"What a good time to go out. Just to see whatever I might find," the wolfdog thought. So, off he went. The great dog found the trail of a rabbit, which he followed. Seeing the white cotton ball at the end of the creature, he bounded after it. But the rabbit was lucky and too quick, eluding the wolfdog and escaping to his underground burrow.

There were many smells in the heat of the day. Which one should he follow? The wolfdog was undecided.

Suddenly, scent made the hairs on his back stand straight up. He knew only too well what it was. It was the scent of a wolf! The great wolfdog trotted in the direction from where the scent was coming. As the scent got stronger, he loped faster, hackles up, anticipating dispatching a hateful creature.

The wolfdog trailed the scent through the woods, and he came to a large clearing where he spied three wolves. The wolves were so busy looking menacingly at a leprechaun family that they did not notice the wolfdog. The leprechaun family was tightly huddled together because they were terrified. A whole family could not escape easily—even with their magical powers.

The great wolfdog leaped in front of the wolves before they realized what was happening. The wolfdog began to attack the lead wolf, driving him away from the little family. The other wolves came in to fight, but the wolfdog turned on them. He was so big, so fast, and so powerful that the wolves began to have second thoughts about their attack on the leprechaun family. Just looking at the wolfdog's great teeth made the other wolves back away. The wolves turned and ran off to lick the wounds suffered by the lead wolf.

The leprechaun family was crying together over what had nearly happened to them. They looked up and saw wounds on their big, furry rescuer. The little people scurried to take care of the places where the wolfdog had been bitten.

As the leprechauns were caring for the wolfdog, they heard the sounds of a small child crying somewhere nearby. To hear more clearly, the wolfdog pulled his ears back. He went to investigate, with the leprechaun family following close behind.

As they came around a big boulder at the edge of the woods, the sound of crying got louder.

It was a child, a little girl the wolfdog had seen before. She had long, shiny, red-gold braids at either side of her head. A garland of wildflowers was just above the braids, and the child was clutching a bunch of lavender and white flowers in her hands. She was the daughter of the prince, who lived in the castle near where the great wolfdog lived.

Suddenly, screams from the child erupted when a burly, and ill-tempered big, hungry bear came out of the woods. The bear stood on its hind feet with his great jaws open showing deadly teeth. He twisted his head back and forth as he emitted a mighty roar while walking toward the little girl.

The child screamed an ear piercing scream, but she was too afraid to run.

The great wolfdog did not hesitate. He leaped into the path of

the great bear, biting it as the bear slashed at the wolfdog with its claws. After the wolfdog stood on his hind feet and bit at the bear, the bear could tell this great animal was too much trouble for him, so he came down on all four feet and stalked off, huffing his way into the woods.

In spite of the fact that the wolfdog was bleeding, he turned and licked the child and lay down beside her.

The leprechaun family had seen this great show of heroism. They put a spell on the child so she would sleep and not see them.

A rainbow appeared in the sky. Its end came to rest near where they all were.

The leprechauns recognized that this was the same great wolfdog who had saved one of theirs from a wild boar.

They knew he had also saved a friend from drowning.

He had just saved them from the wolves. And now the wolfdog had rescued the little girl from the bear.

The leprechauns looked at the wounds on the giant wolfdog's chest from the claws of the bear.

The leprechaun family rushed over to stop the wolfdog's bleeding.

"We have great wealth here at the end of the rainbow. Come with us. We will gladly give it to you," the leprechauns said.

The wolfdog looked at the leprechauns, unwilling to leave the child.

The leprechauns felt they had to do something, so they told the wolfdog that forever, all would know what a brave and noble dog he was. Where his chest had been wounded by the bear, he would be forever more be marked with white.

His children would also be so marked, and his grandchildren, and all of his kind who came after him. The leprechauns hugged the wolfdog, touched his chest three times so that it suddenly had a white splotch on it and skittered away into the mist behind the rainbow.

When the little girl woke up, she did not remember having heard or seen anything about the leprechauns. The giant wolfdog was curled up beside her. She hugged him and wiped her tears on his fur. He responded with warm sloppy kisses.

The girl and the wolfdog both stood, and the dog began to walk to where the child lived.

"I know where she lives," the wolfdog thought. "She is the daughter of the honored Prince of Ireland."

The girl's nurse had fallen asleep while the child was picking flowers to make a garland to take back home. The little girl had not really meant to wander so far and become lost. The nurse was distraught when she awoke and found no child. She had run to the castle, wringing her hands in despair, frantically telling her story to the prince and his followers.

The terrified men and the prince had run into the forest calling the child's name, knowing the many dangers that lurked there. As they came to a clearing, the men spied the little girl walking in their direction and at the same time hugging the great wolfdog. The child ran to her father when she saw him.

"Father, Father, I must tell you all that has happened and how this brave dog saved me from a bear. I did not mean to get lost, but I wandered too far. I am truly sorry."

When they got home, the prince's daughter refused to be separated from the wolfdog. The wolfdog was allowed to come in the castle where he became the child's constant companion.

The next day, there was a great celebration over the child's safe return. The great Prince of Ireland declared the dog the national dog of the land— to be known thereafter as the Irish Wolfhound.

The leprechauns kept their promise. All wolfhounds have some white markings on their toes, the tips of their tail, and their chest.

It was a great tale and told many times, but only the wolfhound knew about the leprechauns and where they kept their great wealth. He thought of them each time he saw a rainbow.

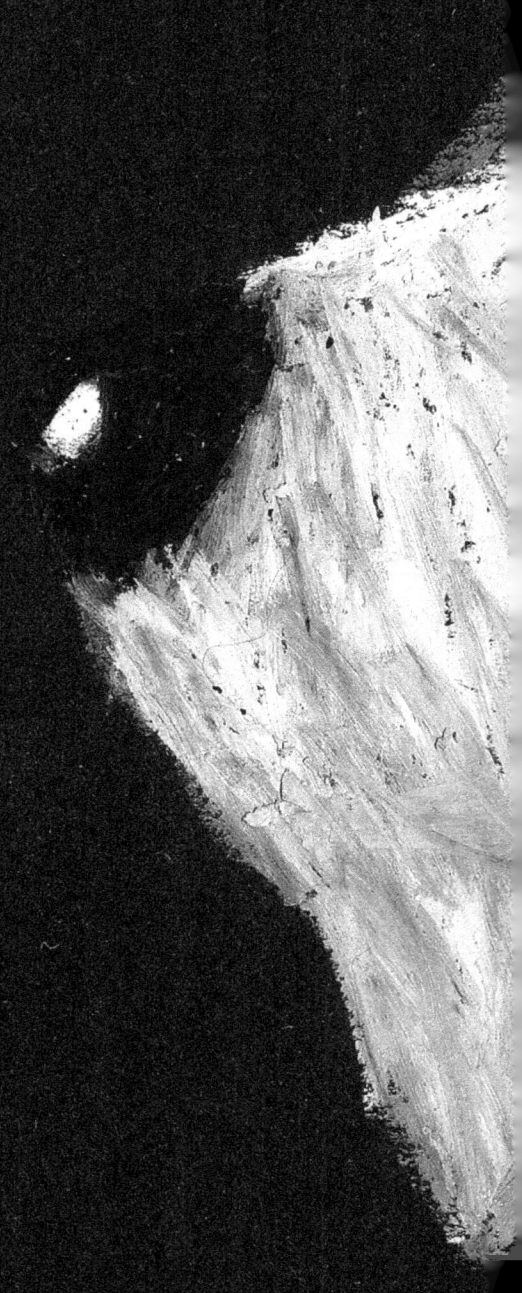

THINGS WE KNOW ABOUT WOLFHOUNDS IN HISTORY

- 🐾 Wolfdogs were known to have been with the Celts during the time they wandered across Europe including in Greece.

- 🐾 Wolfhounds have been found in Iceland, Norway, Sweden, and Russia.

- 🐾 There are written accounts of seven wolfhounds being walked together through the streets of Rome in the year 391 AD. They had been taken to Rome after the Romans invaded England and Wales.

- 🐾 For many years, only royalty was allowed to own a wolfhound. The kings and queens of England would often give them as gifts to special royal friends.

- 🐾 As time went on, they were occasionally given to special people who were not of royal blood. One such exception was an Irish Wolfhound that was given to St. Patrick. Too many were given as gifts, and soon they were on the verge of becoming extinct. But devoted lovers of the Irish Wolfhound saw to it that did not happen. In 1652, a law was passed that no more Irish Wolfhounds could leave Ireland. That law was in effect for many years.

- 🐾 Columbus made many trips to the Americas, and on one of his voyages, he was accompanied by a wolfhound. I am going to guess that Queen Isabella of Spain gave the dog to him to thank him for his sailing explorations.

- An Irish Wolfhound was a companion to the Irish Brigade that was from New York State that fought in the Civil War. The dog died at Gettysburg. There is a statue of a Celtic cross with a wolfhound lying next to it as a tribute in a grove of trees at Gettysburg Battlefield.

- General Custer kept Irish Wolfhounds and Scottish Deerhounds to hunt for him and his troops. There are photographs of him at his home with them and also in front of a teepee where an important meeting took place between Custer and Indians before Custer died.

- In modern times, Ireland gave President Kennedy an Irish Wolfhound when he visited. The dog did not stay at the White House, but it did live in the United States.

- Today, a number of people in Australia have wolfhounds.

- In our very own state of Washington, two different governors have had Irish Wolfhounds that lived in our State Capitol—Governor Daniel Evans and Governor Dixie Lee Ray.

- We who have Irish Wolfhounds feel we are privileged to have such kind, brave, loyal dogs to share our lives with. Alas, it is never long enough.

HOUNDS OF THE HEROES

Huge hound
Great Hound
Gray hound and gaunt
Royally Imperial, you tower above taunt

Comrade of Chieftains
Grim dog of war
Your frame has been heralded
And hailed from afar

From Rome of the Caesars
From Spain's classic bard
You've won kingly praises
And knightly award.

The elk of old Erin
You brought to its knees
At the roar of your challenge
The timber wolf flees.

Yet noble descendant
Of fierce fighting sire
You are playing tonight
With my child by the fire.

Many years ago, a man named William Damerell (1317–1361) wrote this poem about the Irish Wolfhound.

ACKNOWLEDGMENTS

Thank you to my husband, Paul Jackson, for all of his help.

This story came about because my dog Tynan did not like having his nails dremmeled. I had him washed and dremmeled about a month before a show, and while I was waiting I wrote this story because Cherrydale School in Steilacoom, Washington, wanted me to come to the school and tell about Irish Wolfhounds on St. Patrick's Day.

ABOUT THE AUTHOR

Coming home to Irish Wolfhounds for some 50 years, showing them, and being involved with other Irish Wolfhound activities filled out JoAnn Lakin Jackson's busy life as a kindergarten teacher at Cherrydale Primary School in Steilacoom, Washington. Now retired, she shares her life with her husband, Paul, and their Border Terrier, Duggan.

Besides showing her dogs here in the United States, she has put titles on her dogs at Canadian and International shows. She has also attained obedience titles as well as other working titles on her dogs.

While she was teaching, she often adapted well-known children's stories into plays for her students to perform. Since retiring, she has written two collections of short stories, *Unexpected Diversity Tales*, followed by a collection of stories, *Naughty Dog ~~Tails~~ Tales*, written by Duggan himself, with help from JoAnn.

JoAnn and Paul are both writers, belonging to Plateau Area Writer's Association, a writing group in the South Sound area of Puget Sound in Washington State, which is where the two met.

ABOUT THE ARTIST

Kat Moloney started showing Irish Wolfhounds with her dad two years ago. She has two beautiful giants named Selene and Lycan. She also loves creating art and started her journey within the arts during the coronavirus pandemic. After graduating from high school in 2022, she will be attending Pacific Lutheran University, majoring in studio arts and psychology.

CPSIA information can be obtained
at www.ICGtesting.com
Printed in the USA
BVHW010813080323
659705BV00024B/7